Little Book of Fables

Little Book of
Fables

Retold by Verónica Uribe
Translated by Susan Ouriou
Pictures by Constanza Bravo

A Groundwood Book
Douglas & McIntyre
Toronto Vancouver Berkeley

First published in Spanish as EL LIBRO DE ORO DE LAS FÁBULAS
copyright © 2004 by Ediciones Ekaré, Caracas, Venezuela
First published in English by Groundwood Books
English translation copyright © 2004 by Susan Ouriou

Groundwood Books / Douglas & McIntyre
720 Bathurst Street, Suite 500
Toronto, Ontario M5S 2R4

Distributed in the USA by
Publishers Group West
1700 Fourth Street, Berkeley, CA 94710

We acknowledge for their financial support of our publishing program the
Government of Ontario through the Ontario Media Development Corporation's
Ontario Book Initiative.

National Library of Canada Cataloging in Publication
Uribe, Verónica
Little book of fables / retold by Verónica Uribe; pictures by Constanza Bravo;
translation by Susan Ouriou.
Translation of: El libro de oro de las fábulas.
ISBN 0-88899-573-3
I. Bravo, Constanza II. Ouriou, Susan III. Title.
PZ8.2.U74Li 2004   j863   C2004-901351-3

Art direction by Irene Savino
Design by Ivan Larraguibel
Printed and bound in China

Contents

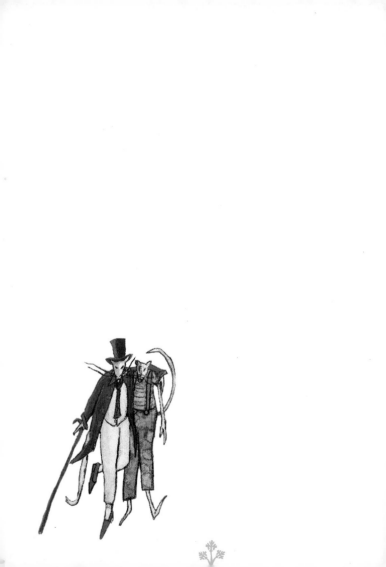

Country Mouse and City Mouse

It had been quite some time since City Mouse visited his cousin Country Mouse, so one day he packed up and set out to see him.

"Cousin! What a surprise!" Country Mouse greeted him with glee. He invited City Mouse into the barn where he lived. In no time, City Mouse's elegant dark suit was covered with straw.

"All this dust and straw!" City Mouse complained, shaking himself off.

"Straw makes a very comfortable bed," said Country Mouse. "Besides, a bit of dust and straw never hurt anyone. But you must be hungry. Let's eat."

He invited his cousin to sit down at the table spread with sunflower seeds, crusts of rye bread and two walnut shells full of milk.

Country Mouse ate with great gusto, but City Mouse complained.

"Such boring food, Cousin! You should see what we eat in the city."

"Fine, some day I'll visit the city and try the food there."

When they had finished their meal, it was time for bed. Country Mouse fell asleep right away, but City Mouse lay awake listening to all the strange sounds. The straw bed made him itchy, and sleep would not come. He shook his cousin awake and asked, "What's that strange noise I hear?"

"Oh," Country Mouse yawned, "those are crickets chirping. A perfect lullaby, don't you think?"

"An annoyance is more like it!" City Mouse complained. He barely got a wink of sleep all night.

Very early the next morning, City Mouse said to Country Mouse, "Cousin, I've decided we should go to my house this very day. There you will see what delicacies we eat and how delightful it is to sleep on a feather bed."

Country Mouse agreed quite happily. "You're

right, Cousin. It's time I saw the city."

And so off they went.

*   *   *

They arrived in the city at the busiest time. The din of traffic and the rush of people made Country Mouse dizzy.

"What a deafening noise!" he complained.

But City Mouse wasn't listening. He was scurrying frantically after the scraps of food people dropped on the ground.

"Please let's go to your house right away. I don't feel very well," Country Mouse begged.

At last they arrived at City Mouse's elegant apartment. It just so happened that the people who lived there were having a party.

"We're in luck, Cousin," City Mouse rejoiced. "This means delicacies to come, just like I told you."

They hid in City Mouse's mouse hole waiting for the guests to leave. Inside was a silk cushion stuffed with feathers so soft and slippery that

Country Mouse slid to the ground every time he tried to climb up onto it.

"This bed is definitely soft, but far from comfortable," he thought to himself.

Finally, much later, when Country Mouse had almost dozed off, City Mouse said, "They're gone! Time for our banquet."

They jumped up onto the table and began feasting on cheese from Holland, ham from Italy, white bread, almond cake and apple pie. They had only just begun nibbling on the sumptuous spread when *whoosh*! A Siamese cat leaped out of nowhere onto the table.

"Watch out!" City Mouse shouted and ran back into the mouse hole.

But Country Mouse was not as quick, and the cat's claws grazed his tail just as he slipped into the hole.

"What a fright! Ouch, my tail really hurts!"

The next day, Country Mouse said good-bye to City Mouse.

"Dear Cousin, thank you for the invitation," he said. "The city is definitely exciting and the food delicious, but all that work for such small pickings! I prefer my seeds, my straw bed and my crickets. Farewell, Cousin!"

To each his own.

The Hen and the Golden Egg

A farmer and his wife bought a hen at market one day. The wife rose very early the next morning to see whether the hen had laid an egg.

What a surprise awaited her! Not only had the hen laid an egg, she had laid an egg like no other – a golden egg!

The hen continued to lay one golden egg every couple of days to the delight and amazement of the farmer and his wife. With money from the eggs, they bought new clothes. They bought animals for their farm and furniture for their house. And they no longer had to work as hard as before.

One morning, however, the husband woke up thinking to himself that two or three days was too long to wait for just one egg. He wanted more golden eggs right away. So he said to his wife, "What a nuisance it is having to wait so long for the hen to lay one measly egg! Wouldn't it be better to kill her, slit open her belly and take out all the eggs at once?"

His wife thought this sounded like a good idea.

So the farmer grabbed a knife and cut open the hen only to find that like any other hen, she had no golden eggs inside.

By asking for more, you often receive less. That is why we say,
"Don't kill the hen (or goose) that lays the golden egg."

The Dog and the Piece of Meat

One day a dog, who prided himself on his cleverness, stole a large piece of meat from a butcher shop.

He ran far away looking for a spot where he could eat the meat in peace. As he crossed a bridge over a deep, slow-moving river, he happened to look down. Seeing his reflection in the water, he thought to himself, "That dog down there has a piece of meat, too. His looks bigger than mine. And that dog doesn't look too bright. I think I'll scare him and have his meat as well as mine. What a clever dog I am!"

But when he opened his mouth to bark, the meat fell out and sank beneath the water out of sight.

Clever is as clever does.

The Lion and the Mosquito

A mosquito woke up one day feeling brave and invincible and wanted to let the whole world know. So he flew to the lion's den, calling out loudly as he went, "I'm invincible! No one can beat me, not even the lion."

The mosquito's boast surprised the other animals. They followed him to see what would happen. When he reached the lion's den, the mosquito said, "Lion, I can beat you. I know I can."

"Mosquito, you're too small to fight me," the lion said, ignoring him.

"I may be small, but I am brave and invincible," the mosquito buzzed. "Let's fight."

"If that's what you want," the lion said.

With a mighty roar, he struck out with his huge paw. But the mosquito ducked under the lion's paw and headed straight for his nose – the most sensitive part of a lion – and bit him again and again.

The frantic lion pawed at his nose and clawed at his hide, but the mosquito was too fast for him. Finally, in desperation, the lion said, "Enough, mosquito, enough. I give up. You win."

The animals applauded, and the mosquito rejoiced. "I am invincible! I am brave! I am the best!"

"You are indeed brave," said the lion. "As for invincible, that's another matter."

But the mosquito didn't even hear the lion as he buzzed off. In his carelessness, he flew straight into a spider's web and got hopelessly entangled.

The spider pounced on him and ate him up.

Cunning and valor may help the weak beat the powerful, but nothing can make them invincible.

The Fox and the Stork

The fox had always maintained that the stork was a fool. One day he decided to play a trick on her.

The fox invited the stork to his house for dinner. He prepared a delicious meal and laid it out on the elegant table he had set. The stork arrived to the mouth-watering aroma of good cooking. But…

When they sat down for dinner, the stork realized that the fox had served all the food on large, flat plates from which it was impossible for her to eat with her long, skinny beak. But she said nothing.

Later, the stork thanked the fox for dinner and left. The fox sat at home and laughed himself silly.

A few days later, they bumped into each other by the pond, and the stork invited the fox over for dinner. The fox accepted the invitation immediately.

He went home laughing to himself, thinking, "That stork is such a fool. She actually wants to repay me for my invitation."

The stork took pains to make a sumptuous meal. The fox arrived right on time, and his mouth started to water at all the tempting smells wafting from the dining room. But…

When they sat down to eat, the fox realized that the stork had served all the food in skinny, long-necked bottles, suitable for a stork's bill but never for a fox's muzzle.

The stork ate to her heart's content. When she had had her fill, she said, "So, Fox? Have I not made a meal for you that is every bit as delicious as the one you made for me?"

Do unto others as you would have them do unto you.

The Milkmaid

A young girl on her way to market carried a jug of milk on her head. As she walked, she began to daydream about the money the milk would bring.

"With the money I make from the milk, I'll buy myself a basket of eggs. I'll let the eggs hatch into four dozen hens. I'll raise the hens in the barnyard and fatten them up on seeds, and then I'll sell them. With the money I earn, I'll buy a piglet. I'll feed it generously until it grows fat and pink. Then I'll sell the pig and buy… a calf! Afterward, I'll sell the calf and buy myself a beautiful dress to wear to town, and all the boys will stare at me. Then I'll toss my head haughtily, like this."

At that, the milkmaid tossed her head, and the jug of milk fell to the ground and broke. "Good-bye milk, good-bye eggs, good-bye hens, good-bye pig… good-bye calf," she thought sadly to herself.

Don't count your chickens before they've hatched.

The Shepherd and the Wolf

One day, for a lark, a shepherd boy decided to shout with all his might, "A wolf is coming! A wolf is coming!"

Farmers working nearby heard his cries and ran to his rescue bearing sticks. But there was no sign of a wolf.

The boy told them that the wolf had run off when it heard them coming. Only partially convinced, the farmers went back to work.

The shepherd boy quite enjoyed the stir he had caused. A few days later, he felt the urge to cry out again, "A wolf is coming! A wolf is coming!"

Once again the farmers ran uphill to his rescue. But as with the first time, there was no sign of a wolf. The farmers scolded the boy and went back down the hill in a very bad mood.

Two days later, a wolf appeared. The shepherd

boy was terrified and shouted desperately, "Wolf! Wolf! Help!"

The farmers, thinking it was just another trick, kept on working and paid no attention to him.

The wolf killed three sheep from the shepherd boy's flock.

No one believes a liar, even when he speaks
the truth.

The Lion and the Mouse

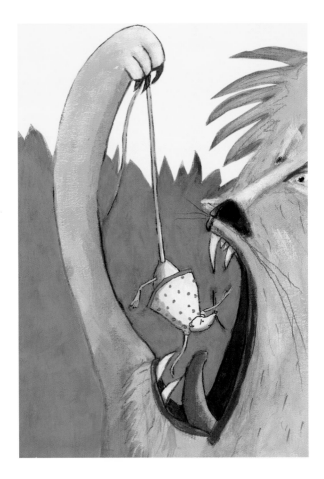

One day a mouse was out walking, not paying attention to where he was going, and he accidentally walked right up over a lion taking a nap.

The lion felt something tickling his back and reached over to scratch himself.

"What's this?" he said, feeling the mouse. He scooped the mouse up in his huge paw and brought him closer for a better look. "Well, what do you know," the lion growled. Then he opened his huge jaws to swallow the poor mouse.

Just before the trembling mouse disappeared into the lion's mouth, he managed to speak.

"Mr. Lion, Mr. Lion, please spare me, and one day I will save your life."

This seemed to amuse the lion. He laughed out loud.

"What a funny idea. Imagine you being capable of saving my life one day — me, the king of the jungle," he said. "You've made me laugh, little mouse. I'll let you go."

Still laughing, he released the mouse, and the mouse fled.

* * *

Months passed, during which the mouse stayed clear of the lion's territory. One day, however, he heard cries in the distance. He followed the pitiful sound and found the lion caught in a rope net. A trap had been set to capture him.

"Mr. Lion," the mouse said. "Some time ago I promised I would save your life one day. Today is that day." And he began gnawing at the net until the lion was set free.

The grateful lion said, "I would never have thought that someone as tiny as you could help me — let alone save my life."

Little friends may prove to be great friends.

A Man, His Son and Their Donkey

A man set out on a trip with his son and their donkey. His son sat on the donkey's back while he walked along beside them.

They passed through a town. People stared at them and said, "Did you see that? That strong, young boy is riding the donkey while his aging father has to walk."

Hearing this, the man swung his son off the donkey and got on in his place. On they went.

They passed through another town. People stared at them and said, "Can you believe that! The man rides on the donkey like a king while his little boy grows weary running by his side."

Hearing this, the man got off the donkey, and both father and son walked, leading the donkey by the reins.

They passed through another town. People stared at them and said, "What fools to walk when they have a donkey they could ride!"

Hearing this, the man put his son on the donkey and got up behind him.

They passed through another town. People stared at them and said, "How cruel, to make that poor animal carry the weight of two!"

Hearing this, the man got off the donkey then took his son down. They found some rope and a big stick, tied the donkey's legs together, and hung the donkey from the stick. Then they started walking again, carrying the donkey.

They passed through another town and people laughed. "Did you see that? Talk about crazy! A man and a child carrying a donkey."

By this time, the man was very angry. He set the donkey down on the ground, untied its legs and put his son on the donkey's back.

"This is the way I left home, and this is the way I will continue," he said.

Please all and you will please none.

The Tortoise and the Hare

One day a hare met up with a tortoise. "You are so slow, Tortoise," the hare said. "I, on the other hand… watch me." In one second flat, the hare ran to the end of the field and back.

"You are swift," the tortoise agreed.

"Look at the crooked legs on you," said the hare. "You can't run on those."

"No, I never run. I just walk, slow and steady," said the tortoise. "But I'd like to challenge you to a race."

"A race?" the hare laughed. "A race between you and me?"

"Yes. Between the two of us," the tortoise replied.

The hare thought this was the funniest thing he had ever heard, and he agreed. They appointed the owl as their referee and decided on a time for the race.

All the animals of the forest came to watch. The owl marked the course and gave the starting signal.

The hare shot off. Halfway to the finish line, he looked back and saw that the tortoise had only covered a few yards. He thought, "Seeing how long it will take the tortoise to get this far, I have plenty of time to help myself to some carrots in the field."

The hare left the track and ate many carrots in the nearby field. When he returned to the track, he looked behind him again. The tortoise had covered a few more yards but was still a long way away.

"I have time for a rest," said the hare. He lay down under the shade of a tree. Feeling sleepy from the heat and having eaten more than his fill, he dozed off.

The tortoise kept on walking, slow and steady, without pause. At the same slow and steady pace, he passed the sleeping hare. And slow and steady, he headed toward the finish line. It was very hot, and the tortoise was thirsty, but he did not stop.

Suddenly, the hare woke up. He looked behind him but could see no sign of the tortoise.

"Where did he go?" he thought. Then he looked toward the finish line and saw that the tortoise was about to cross. The hare ran as fast as his legs could carry him. But the tortoise crossed the finish line before the hare could catch up.

The owl decreed the tortoise the winner, and all the animals of the forest were astonished at the outcome of the race.

Slow and steady wins
the race

The Old Lion and the Wary Foxes

A lion, who was well on in years and tired of hunting, pretended to be sick. Then he asked the animals of the forest to visit him in his cave.

He took advantage of the most gullible animals who ventured into the dark cave, and he killed and ate every one.

One day, having heard of the lion's illness, the foxes stopped at the entrance to the cave to say hello.

"Are you feeling better, Lion?" they asked.

"A little," the lion replied. "But come closer. Don't stay out in the sun."

"We'd rather stay here," the foxes said.

"Why is that?" the lion asked.

"Because we see many footprints going into the cave, but no footprints coming out."

Trust not an old enemy.

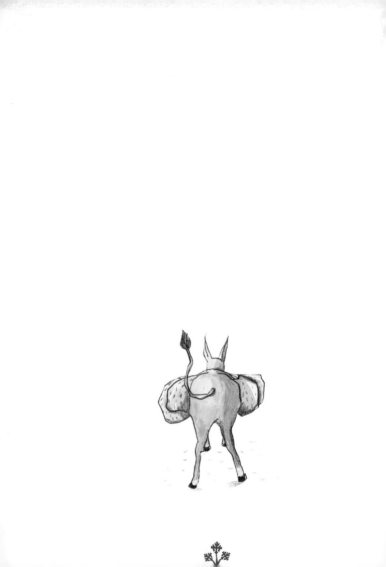

The Donkey and the Salt

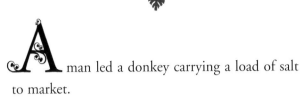

Aman led a donkey carrying a load of salt to market.

They came to a spot where they had to ford a river. The river was high, so the man searched until he found a good place to cross. He stepped into the water with the donkey, but the current was strong, and the donkey had trouble making any headway. When they were almost halfway across, the man realized the river was deeper than he had thought. The donkey had trouble keeping its footing, and its load was getting wet.

But just when the donkey seemed about to drown, it regained its balance and managed to cross as though it had nothing on its back.

The donkey was thrilled to feel so light and ignored the man who complained about having lost more than half his load of salt, which had dissolved in the water.

Further on, they met up with another man going in the opposite direction. He was leading a donkey carrying a load of sponges.

"Be careful crossing the river," the first man warned the second man.

But the first donkey told the second donkey, "Don't worry if you cross the river at its deepest point. As soon as the water reaches your packs, their weight will disappear as if by magic."

The second donkey thought this sounded like good advice. As soon as they reached the river, it ignored its master and started crossing.

But… there was no magic. As soon as the water reached the sponges, they grew heavy and water-logged, and the current swept the donkey away.

A donkey's advice is worse than no advice at all.

The Miser

A very rich and miserly man grew tired of forever being asked for money or favors. And so he decided to sell everything he owned in exchange for gold coins. He put all his gold into a chest, then took the chest to a secret spot by the trunk of a big, old tree and buried it.

Every day he visited his treasure. He sat under the shade of the tree and dreamed about all the gold coins buried safely underground.

One day, however, a man secretly followed him. He heard the miser talking to himself, singing his hidden treasure's praise and gleefully patting the ground, as though showing the place his fortune lay buried.

As soon as the miser left, the man dug up the treasure and carried it away.

The next day, the miser found nothing but a hole under the tree. He was beside himself, weeping and wailing, tearing at his hair and beating his chest with his fists.

Seeing the state he was in, a friend said, "Go find yourself a rock and bury it in that same spot. Pretend it is your treasure and visit it every day. The rock will be just as useful as your gold was where it lay buried and unused."

What good is it to own something if you do not enjoy it?

Belling the Cat

The mice had been worried ever since the farmer bought the cat. They could no longer roam freely, or catch a ray of sun whenever they felt like it, or eat a leisurely meal.

They decided to hold a meeting to discuss the problem. Life had become much too dangerous.

"What can be done about it?" the mice asked each other.

No one had the slightest idea, until a little mouse said, "The cat is very quiet, isn't he?"

"That's so, that's so," the others said.

"We can never hear him creeping up on us," said the little mouse.

"True, true," all the others said.

"Well then," the little mouse continued, "we should put a bell on the cat."

"A bell?" the astonished mice asked.

"Yes, we should bell the cat. That way, whenever he's near, we'll hear it ringing and have time to run away."

"What a wonderful idea!" one mouse said.

"Brilliant!" said another.

"That's our solution. We're saved," they chorused.

"Wait a minute, now," said the oldest mouse of all. "Tell me, who will bell the cat?"

It is easy to propose impossible remedies.
That is why we say, "Who will bell the cat?" if someone
comes up with an unworkable solution.

The Fox and the Grapes

One day when a fox went for a walk in the countryside, he noticed a grapevine. Nestled in its leaves was a large bunch of grapes. They looked ripe and as soft as velvet.

"Such big, fat grapes! I bet they're juicy and sweet," the fox said, licking his chops.

Since the vine hung high above his head, he tried standing on his back legs to reach it. But it was still too high. He gave a little jump. Again, no luck. The fox leaped three, four times, each time more energetically. But he still could not reach the bunch of grapes.

Finally, the fox turned his back on the grapes and continued on his way.

"Who wants sour grapes anyway?" he muttered.

It is easy to scorn what you cannot get.
That is why we say "Sour grapes" when we hear someone speak
disdainfully of something they cannot do.

91

The Reed and the Oak

A luxuriant oak tree stood next to a lagoon. At the water's edge nearby grew a slender green reed. The two talked from time to time, although the oak did most of the talking.

"Do you see, Little Reed, how thick my branches are? And how dense and green my leaves?"

"Yes, Oak," the reed answered. "Your foliage is indeed magnificent."

The oak rustled its leaves as it swayed in the breeze. "I've grown so much this year. All the rain and sunlight have made me big and strong."

"That they have," said the reed. "You look vibrant and majestic."

"Let the storm clouds gather, let the hurricanes blow," said the oak. "I'm not afraid because I'm strong. I can stand up to the winds and resist their force. You, on the other hand, poor little reed, so small and slight, what will become of you in a storm?"

"I don't know," said the reed. "I've never been through one."

That very night a terrible storm blew in, unleashing wind and rain. The oak fought the hurricane with its thick trunk and strong branches. It never yielded to the force of the wind. But halfway through the storm, a particularly violent gust of wind knocked the oak tree over and tore its roots from the ground.

The reed, on the other hand, put up no resistance. As long as the wind blew, the reed bent before it, almost grazing the water again and again.

The next morning the oak lay dead on the ground, and the reed swayed gently in the breeze.

Not all battles can be fought head on.

The Stag with Beautiful Antlers

One morning a stag, drinking from a pond, saw his reflection in the water. He thought to himself, "What beautiful antlers I have. Don't I look elegant? But my legs are a sorry sight in contrast! So spindly and bony."

The stag was still admiring his antlers when he heard the baying of hunters' dogs. He dashed away from the pond and ran to hide in the woods. His legs carried him swiftly and surely, but as he passed under a leafy tree, his antlers got caught in its branches.

The stag tried to free his antlers, but each time he shook his head, the more entangled he became. The dogs were closing in on him. The stag gave one last, desperate tug and managed to free himself.

Once he was in the woods and able to catch his breath, he thought, "The antlers I admired so much nearly killed me, while the legs I hated so much saved my life."

What is truly valuable is often unappreciated.

The Fox and the Crow

One morning a crow settled on the branch of a tree to eat a piece of cheese he had found.

A fox passing by saw the cheese and said to the crow, "O Crow, how handsome you are! Such sleek, black feathers!"

The crow was startled by the fox's praise. He spread his wings, looked at his feathers, and saw that they were indeed lovely and sleek.

"O Crow," the fox continued. "How I love watching you soar through the air!"

The proud crow took wing and flew a few circles in the air as the fox watched. Then he returned to his branch.

"I do indeed cut quite an elegant figure," he thought to himself. "The fox is right."

"O Crow," the fox spoke again. "Given how handsome your feathers are and how you fly like the king of the sky, what a beautiful song you must sing."

The crow thought that his voice was really something special.

"O Crow, won't you sing for me?" pleaded the fox.

Flattered, the crow decided to do just that. He opened his beak and out fell the cheese.

The fox caught the cheese in midair and gulped it down.

Beware of those who flatter unduly.

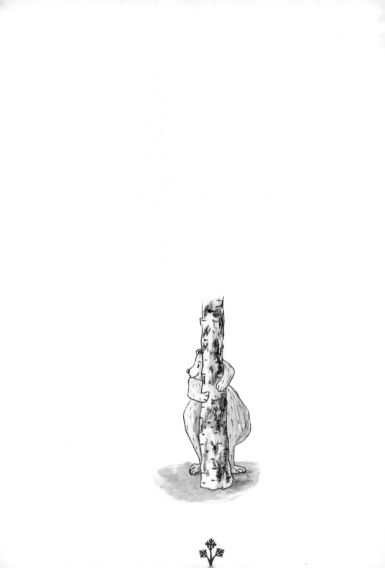

The Two Friends and the Bear

Two young friends were walking through a dense forest when suddenly they heard the footsteps of an animal close by.

"A bear!" they whispered in fright.

The more nimble of the two boys shinned up a tree and hid among the leaves. His friend, who was slow and clumsy, tried to follow suit but could not.

"Help me, please!" he begged. But his friend was too busy hiding to answer him.

By that time the bear was almost upon them, so the boy fell to the ground and played dead. He knew that a bear would never eat a dead animal. There he lay, as quiet as could be, despite the terror he felt.

The bear drew near and began sniffing at his legs, his back, his neck and his ears. The boy felt the animal graze his hair, but he held his breath to deceive the bear.

Finally, the bear lumbered off.

The boy's friend climbed down from his hiding place and said, "It looked like the bear said something to you. What did he whisper in your ear?"

"He gave me good advice."

Full of curiosity, the nimble boy asked, "What good advice was that?"

"He told me never to travel with a friend who abandons me when danger is near."

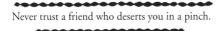

Never trust a friend who deserts you in a pinch.

The North Wind and the Sun

The north wind boasted that he was very strong. He told the sun, "I can throw down trees and destroy houses and make them fly like feathers in the air. Nobody matches my strength. When I blow, all bend."

"There are many ways of being strong," said the sun.

Just then, they saw a man walking down the road. The sun said, "I know how to settle our argument. Whoever makes the man take off his cloak will be the strongest one."

"All right," said the north wind. "That will be easy for me to do."

"You go first," the sun said.

The sun hid behind a cloud, and the north wind began to blow. It swirled around the traveler, and the man shivered as his cloak flew into the air. The wind blew harder. The man hunched over to meet the force of the gale and wrapped his cloak around him. The harder the north wind blew, the tighter the man held on to his cloak.

The north wind grew tired and said to the sun, "Let us see what you can do."

"Let us see," said the sun and began to shine.

The man straightened up and let go of his cloak. The sun shone brightly on his path. The man felt the rays of the sun warming his body. Soon the heat was so great that the man took off his cloak.

The north wind blew away, defeated, and the sun continued to shine.

Persuasion is better than force.

About Aesop and the Fables

AESOP

The slave Aesop was an ugly man, and he was hopeless as a worker. He was frail and had arms too short and a head too big for his body. He had bow legs, crooked feet, a pot belly, and he was cross-eyed. To add to his misfortunes, he was mute. But the goddess Isis cured him by giving him the power of speech, which Aesop used to demonstrate his cleverness, earn his freedom and become an adviser to kings.

This is how Aesop is described in *Life of Aesop*, one of the first anonymous picaresque texts thought to relate the life of the famous Greek fabulist. According to manuscripts that have survived to the present day, *Life of Aesop* was written circa 100 B.C.

Whether or not this description of Aesop is true to life is impossible to know. Some people even wonder whether Aesop was a real person or a literary character. But there are some facts about Aesop's life on which many people agree: he was born a slave in Phrygia, a region of Asia Minor, and lived in the second half of the sixth century B.C. His knowledge and cleverness earned him his freedom, and he became an adviser to King Croesus in Lydia. In court, he made the acquaintance of Thales, Solon and other philosophers. He traveled to Babylon, to Egypt and to several cities in the Greek peninsula. In Delphi, where he was sent as Croesus' ambassador, he was falsely accused of stealing a goblet from the temple and sentenced to death. Legend has it that Zeus was so angry with the inhabitants of Delphi for executing Aesop that he sent plagues and calamities upon them until they repented and built a statue in Aesop's honor.

THE FABULISTS

The first known fables came from Mesopotamia. From there, they traveled east and west. In Greece, Hesiod, Aeschylus and Archilochus cultivated the genre, and in India, the Panchatantra carried on the fabulist tradition.

Aesop was not the first person to write fables, but he was the most popular fabulist and the one who gave the genre its classic form – a brief tale that teaches a lesson. His fables, transmitted orally, were used in ancient Greece as exercises in rhetoric and grammar.

Philosophers had their students memorize and recite the fables, and urged them to come up with their own versions. According to Plato, while Socrates was in prison, he kept himself occupied by versifying Aesop's fables.

The fables were transcribed into Greek prose circa 300 B.C. by Demetrius Phalereus. In the first century A.D., they were transcribed into Latin iambic verse by Phaedrus. Aphthonius, a rhetoricist from Antioch, wrote the fables in prose in 315 A.D. Much later, in the fourteenth century, Maximus Planudes, a monk from Constantinople, collected 150 fables attributed to Aesop and accompanied the text to these stories with *Life of Aesop*, the picaresque text mentioned above.

After the invention of the printing press, Planudes' manuscript was one of the first to be published by Bonus Accursius in 1475. The first Spanish edition was printed by Johan Hurus in Zaragoza, in 1489, and bore the title *Esta es la vida del Ysopet con sus fábulas historyadas*. Since that time, Aesop's fables have been translated into many languages and continue to be reissued, forming part of the literary culture of many different countries.

Over the centuries the genre has been cultivated by a number of authors including Babrius, Phaedrus, Planudes, Marie de France, the archpriest of Hita, Don

Juan Manuel, Jean de la Fontaine, Tomás de Iriarte, Félix María Samaniego and many others to the present day. Almost all were inspired by Aesop's fables in creating their own versions or in inventing new fables.

MORALITY TALES

A fable is a short tale, generally featuring animals, that has an implicit lesson. The tale is almost always comprised of one single action, and the narration is spare, with few details or descriptions.

The protagonists of a fable can be gods, humans, animals or natural elements such as the trees, the sun or the wind. The majority of fables, however, and the most popular ones, feature animals.

Aesop's fables did not include an explicitly stated moral since the lesson was felt to flow naturally from the tale. Other fabulists, however, have felt the need to make the moral of the story clear by adding an admonishing verse or sentence at the beginning or end of the tale.

One reason why fables may have been so popular over the centuries, and used so often to teach children, is because they are morality tales. But the genre has had its detractors. Rousseau, for instance, maintained that "children do not understand fables" and that "the moral of the fables corrupts youth by showing them that the strongest and cleverest are those who win in the end."

The Fables in This Little Book

The twenty fables featured here were chosen for their inherent charm as amusing and popular stories known to many in one version or another. The lessons derived from them have been adopted by cultures the world over and are reflected in popular sayings such as "Who will bell the cat?" or "Don't kill the goose that lays the golden egg" or "Slow and steady wins the race."

Fifteen of the twenty fables here were originally Aesop's, although other fabulists have created their own versions of them as well. Of the remaining five, "Country Mouse and City Mouse" appears in the Babrius collection of fables under the title "El ratón campesino y el ciudadano." "The Fox and the Stork" is one of Phaedrus' fables. "The Milkmaid" comes from Félix María Samaniego and follows on an earlier version by Don Juan Manuel entitled "Lo que sucedió a una mujer llamada Doña Truhana," the only difference being that the woman described by Don Juan Manuel carries a jar of honey and not a jug of milk. "The Cat and the Bell" and "A Man, His Son and Their Donkey" are fables by Jean de la Fontaine.

Traditionally, all those who retell a fable are free to create their own version, and we have been true to that tradition in this book.

V.U.